The 210th Day

Sōseki Natsume (1867–1916) is widely considered the foremost novelist of the Meiji period (1868–1914). After graduating from Tokyo Imperial University in 1893, Sōseki taught high school before spending two years in England on a Japanese government scholarship. He returned to lecture in English literature at the university. Numerous nervous disorders forced him to give up teaching in 1908 and he became a full-time writer for the *Asahi* newspaper. In addition to fourteen novels, Sōseki wrote haiku, poems in the Chinese style, academic papers on literary theory, essays, autobiographical sketches and fairy tales.

Sammy I. Tsunematsu is founder and curator of the Sōseki Museum in London, and the translator of several of Sōseki's works. He has also researched and published widely on the Japanese artist Yoshio Markino, who was a contemporary of Sōseki's living in London at the beginning of the twentieth century. Tsunematsu has lived in Surrey, England, for nearly thirty years.

Sōseki Natsume
The 210th Day

Translated by Sammy I. Tsunematsu

With an Introduction by Marvin Marcus

TUTTLE PUBLISHING
Boston • Rutland, Vermont • Tokyo

Published by Tuttle Publishing
an imprint of Periplus Editions (HK) Ltd,
with editorial offices at 153 Milk Street, Boston, Massachusetts, 01209 and
130 Joo Seng Road, #06-01/03, Singapore 368357.

Originally published in Japanese as *Nihyaku Toka*, 1915
English translation © Sammy I. Tsunematsu, 2002
First Tuttle edition, 2002

Library of Congress Cataloging Card No. 2002102259
ISBN 0 8048 3320 6

The Translator would like to acknowledge the assistance of
John Edmondson who kindly read through the English version
and made many helpful changes.

Printed in Singapore

Distributed by:

North America, Latin America & Europe
Tuttle Publishing
Airport Industrial Park, 364 Innovation Drive
North Clarendon, VT 05759-9436
Tel: (802) 773 8930; Fax: (802) 773 6993

Japan & Korea
Tuttle Publishing
Yaekari Bldg., 3F
5-4-12 Osaki, Shinagawa-ku
Tokyo 141-0032
Tel: (03) 5437 0171; Fax: (03) 5437 0755

Asia Pacific
Berkeley Books Pte Ltd
130 Joo Seng Road, #06-01/03, Singapore 368357
Tel: (65) 6280 1330; Fax: (65) 6280 6290

Contents

Introduction   7

The 210th Day   16

Plates between pp 48 & 49

Introduction

Sōseki Natsume (1867–1916) is a Japanese icon. A native of the great shôgunal capital of Edo, Sōseki was one year old when the Meiji Restoration established Japan as a modern nation and the city of his birth was renamed Tokyo. His lifetime almost perfectly overlaps the course of Japan's extraordinary modernization in the Meiji era (1868–1912). By the time of Sōseki's death in 1916, Japan had become an Asian empire. Not quite seventy years later, Sōseki's face would adorn the national currency, in the form of the 1000-yen banknote.

Sōseki Natsume was one of a handful of writer-intellectuals whose lives and work came to epitomize the age in which they lived—an age that resonates powerfully among Japanese and those with an interest in Japan. Like many of his contemporaries, Sōseki lived at a crossroads where his East Asian cultural heritage and taste for "traditional" arts and styles intersected with a passion for modern intellectual inquiry and knowledge of the West. Initially schooled in the Chinese classics, Sōseki was among the first students at the Imperial University to major in English. He went on to specialize in English literature and spent two years in England at the turn of the century, immersed in literary study.

Sōseki Natsume's mastery of English literature and modern literary theory was unsurpassed when he returned to Japan and assumed a prestigious academic position at the Imperial University. There was every reason to believe that the young scholar would find a comfortable niche at the university. However, the stultifying academic routine proved irksome, and his own literary creations were beginning to earn him a widespread reputation.

The budding author, who had experienced serious melancholia and depression during his stay overseas, was a man of peevish, dyspeptic temperament—a quality reflected both in his fiction and his assorted personal writings. Indeed, Sōseki's assorted neuroses have long been a fixture of modern Japanese literary lore and the subject of endless biographical study and speculation over the years.

Gradually souring on academic life, Sōseki took the unprecedented step of accepting a position with the *Asahi shinbun*, a leading newspaper, as staff writer. By this time, he had already published two remarkable novels—*Wagahai wa Neko de aru* (I am a Cat, 1905), a brilliantly sardonic portrayal of human pecadilloes, as narrated by the family cat; and *Botchan* (1906), a loosely autobiographical account of the youthful experiences of its memorable protagonist.

The *Asahi* position, which Sōseki assumed in

1907, called for the writing of *shinbun shôsetsu*—so-called "newspaper fiction"—which entailed daily serialization of one's work. For a decade, this work would be part of the regular reading diet of the nation's readers, and in due course he emerged as Japan's "novelist-laureate". His mature works—most notably *Kokoro* (1914) and *Michikusa* (Grass on the Wayside, 1915)—are undisputed masterpieces of modern Japanese fiction.

Sōseki Natsume's greatest achievement is perhaps his brilliant psychological portrayal. Acutely sensitive to the spiritual and psychic toll of modern urban existence, Sōseki created a narrative means of evoking the loneliness, alienation and confusion of his protagonists. These are ordinary people leading ordinary lives, yet painfully aware of the barriers of ego and selfishness that enclosed them. Underlying the novels also is the author's enduring concern for the ethical and moral tenor of modern life.

Taken together, the Sōseki novels—serialized at the rate of approximately one per year—possess a Dickensian weight as a collective portrayal of the Meiji era seen through a series of "representative lives".

In addition to the novels, Sōseki wrote widely in other genres—poetry, literary criticism, personal essays, and assorted shorter fiction. The present work, *The 210th Day*, belongs to this latter category. This is a relatively minor work, which has long been overshadowed by the novels. As short fiction, it lacks the sustained plot of *I am* a *Cat* and the character development of *Botchan*. Given the enormous promise of what came before, it almost appears to be a retrograde work.

Yet, seen in its proper context, *The 210th Day* can be appreciated as an intriguing literary experiment, one that reflects the influence of earlier Japanese literary narrative while advancing a distinctly modern and progressive social ideal. It should be noted that the late Meiji period witnessed an outpouring of writing that promoted diverse social, cultural and artistic programs. Sōseki was but one of many writers experimenting with literary avenues for giving voice to prevailing intellectual and ethical issues. Contesting styles were aired in the literary periodicals, and much of this writing will strike the reader as rather awkward and tentative.

The 210th Day is such a work. It takes the form of an extended dialogue, carried over several episodes, between two friends touring the region around the volcanic Mt Aso in central Kyûshû. The work is based on an actual trip that Sōseki made to Kyûshû in September 1899 with a close friend, Yamakawa Shinjirô (1867–?). The two did indeed set out to climb Mt Aso, when they encountered a storm on the "210th day"—which is to say, the lunar calendar day traditionally associated with storms and typhoons.

The two friends in our tale, Kei and Roku, are loosely modeled, respectively, upon Sōseki and Yamakawa. The bulk of the story consists of their rambling dialogue, which proceeds in the absence of any narrative stage-setting. The dialogue is interspersed with occasional descriptions of the inn where they stay; and, later on, the dark, foreboding scenery they encounter on their abortive climb.

Much of this dialogue is marked by easy-going, light-hearted banter. For instance, there is the scene in Chapter 3 involving a somewhat dim-witted waitress who, when asked for some soft-boiled eggs (which in Japanese translates as "half-boiled"), brings out a combination of raw and hard-boiled eggs:

"[Waitress], you can see that the other gentle-man has raw eggs and I have hard-boiled eggs."

"Yes, for sure."

"Why have you done it like that?"

"I boiled half of them."

Such comic patter is redolent of the literary burlesques of the late Tokugawa period (1600–1868) and the popular raconteurs whose lively storytelling captivated Sōseki in his youth. Indeed, the preponderance of dialogue in *The 210th Day* can be interpreted both as homage to an admired cultural form that was on the decline and as a literary étude—an occasion for experimenting with styles of dialogue. The dialogue is indeed quite effective.

The two characters—acquaintances whose relationship remains unclear—contrast strongly with one another. Kei, dynamic and opinionated, lets on that he is the son of a tofu manufacturer, then surprises his friend by advocating a radical social agenda. Proclaiming the need for a just society, Kei expresses disdain for worldly gain and class inequity, and contempt for those with power and privilege. His shrill idealism masks a deeply cynical nature:

"Underneath their congenial masks, human beings are capable of every kind of baseness. If they are penniless they stick to themselves. But if they have a certain position in society, that's when the problems start. They infect the whole of society with their meanness…." (Chapter 3)

Kei's righteous indignation, with which he harangues his easy-going friend, is reminiscent of *I am a Cat*, in which the pretensions of the high and mighty come in for frequent drubbing. A similar moral agenda marks *Botchan*, whose entirely unpretentious protagonist stands up to arrogance, deceit, and hypocrisy. On the other hand, Roku is intrigued by the revelation of his friend's background and wants to hear more. But Kei will not oblige. Their conversation becomes a series of dodges and feints, much like the circuitous path they take up the volcano.

Sōseki sets his tale in the rural hinterland, far from his comfortable urban haunts, and the ensuing description of the hostile elements and ominous natural forces that beset his characters is skillfully drawn:

"The gigantic mountain rumbles more violently every five minutes, and each time the rain and the smoke seem to be quivering in unison, the final waves of vibration shaking the body of Roku, who remains motionless and deprived of strength. As far as the eye can see the grass bends under the smoke and is whipped to and fro by the bursts of rain." (Chapter 4)

The 210th-day storm overpowers the two friends and they must abandon their climb. The next morning, Kei tries to talk his reluctant friend into making another go at climbing Mt Aso. He is intent on having his way. They talk things over, and Kei once again turns to the theme of injustice and the evils wrought by society's high and mighty:

"If we live in this world our foremost aim should be to defeat the monsters of civilization and give some little comfort to the lower classes without money or power; do you not think so?"

"Yes, that's true—yes."

Having finally convinced his friend on this score, Kei uses his leverage to have the friend agree to join him on a second attempt to climb the mountain. And so the story ends.

Kei's discourse on social injustice in *The 210th Day* resonates with the author's own social philosophy, and it reflects the larger concerns of Japanese writers and intellectuals who sought a high moral and intellectual plane for literature. Yet, Sōseki's little tale is as much a parody of intellectual posturing and pomposity as it is a serious presentation of ideas. Its nicely deployed comic effects place it firmly in the orbit of the truly masterful *I am a Cat*.

In a sense, Sōseki's freedom to experiment with

fictional technique, as represented by works such as *The 210th Day*, ended when he joined the *Asahi* staff as a literary journalist. He would now be expected to produce works that appealed to the general reading public. It may be argued that the discourse style employed in his ephemeral "dialogue-tale" would be put to use in the subsequent novels. It is certainly the case that a number of his protagonists would hold forth on social issues and ethics. In this sense, *The 210th Day* stands as an interesting narrative hybrid, written at a particular juncture in the author's career that points to earlier influences while foreshadowing the noteworthy development of his mature literary style.

The present volume is one of the more recent in Tuttle's project of new and reissued translations of Sōseki's work. Thanks to Tuttle, we have a representative sampling of the writings—novelistic and otherwise—of this seminal author, who continues to inspire and entertain Japanese and non-Japanese readers alike. In particular, I am delighted that in addition to *The 210th Day*, Tuttle has recently published several volumes of Sōseki's personal writings, including *Inside My Glass Doors* and *Spring Miscellany*. These collections, which provide fascinating insights into the author's early years, his family, and his circle of friends and colleagues, are a most welcome addition to the work available in English.

MARVIN MARCUS
February 2002

The 210ᵗʰ Day

Chapter I

Kei returns from somewhere, his arms swinging.

"Where have you been?"

"I went for a little walk in the town."

"Anything to look at?"

"A temple."

"What else?"

"A gingko at the door of the temple."

"And what else?"

"Between the gingko and the main pavilion the road was tiled over for about a hundred meters. The temple is a long, narrow building."

"Did you go in?"

"I gave up the idea."

"Nothing else apart from that?"

"Nothing in particular. There is a temple in most villages, isn't there?"

"Yes, wherever people die, it's certainly needed."

"Certainly," Kei replied, bending his head. Every now and then Kei would express untimely admiration. After a moment he raised his head and declared:

"After that I called on the farrier, who was busy shoeing a horse: you wouldn't believe what an expert job he was making of it."

"I did think you had been gone a long time just to visit a temple. Is it such a rare sight, a horse's shoes being changed?"

"It's not that it's so rare, but I looked on. How many instruments would you say one needed for that?"

"Well, how many?"

"Have a guess."

"We're not going to play guessing games. Tell me, how many?"

"Just imagine, it can't be done with fewer than seven."

"As many as that? What, for instance?"

"What, for instance? Well, at all events, I'm certain of it. First of all, you need a chisel to get rid of the callus. Then a hammer to drive in the chisel. And then a little knife to file off the callus. And a funny gadget for hollowing out the horseshoe. And then…."

"Then what?"

"Then, there are a number of curious things. First of all, I was surprised to see that the horse was so quiet. No matter how one filed away and hollowed out the shoes he remained calm."

"It's only hard skin. Human beings remain placid when they cut their nails."

"Human beings, perhaps. But this was a horse."

"Man or horse, we're just talking about a nail. You certainly seem to have ample time on your hands."

"It's precisely because I have time to spare that I watched. But it's most enjoyable watching red-hot iron being beaten in the half-light. It gives off sparks in all directions."

"Oh yes—even in the very center of Tokyo it makes sparks."

"It may perhaps make sparks in the center of Tokyo, but it's different. First of all, with a farrier up in the mountains, like here, the sound is not the same. And you can hear it from here."

The early autumn sun is sinking behind distant landscapes, the cool of evening is at hand, and while the air of the desolate mountain village brings a melancholy dusk in its wake, a constant clash of iron on iron can be heard.

"You can hear it, can't you?" Kei asks.

"Yes," Roku replies in laconic tones before lapsing into silence.

In the next room two people are conducting a lively conversation.

"And then the other combatant dropped his bamboo saber and was struck on his forearm."

"Oh, I see: he finally suffered a hit on his forearm?"

"Yes a 'touch' on his forearm. But you see, as he had dropped his saber there was nothing more he could do."

"Oh—he dropped his saber?"

"But he had dropped it already."

"If he had dropped it and then received a hit on his forearm, he was in serious trouble."

"He was certainly in trouble. Since he lost his saber and suffered a hit on his arm."

The two men's conversation might go on and

on, coming back again and again to the saber and the forearm. Kei and Roku, seated face to face, glance at each other with a smile.

The constant sound of iron being beaten—a piercing and somewhat disturbing note—pervaded the tranquil village.

"A horse is still being shod. It's turned rather cold, don't you think?" Kei enquired, growing stiff under his white *yukata*.[1] Roku refastens the collar of his unlined kimono, also white, and moves his casually parted knees properly together. Then Kei declares:

"In the very middle of the district where I lived in my childhood there was a tofu[2] seller."

"A tofu seller—so what about it?"

"Well, past the corner of the shop at this tofu seller, a hundred meters further on, was the temple of Kankei."

"The temple of Kankei?"

"Yes. It should still be there. From the door of the temple there was only a bamboo grove to be seen, and it looked as if there was neither a central pavilion nor a priest's residence. In this temple, somebody came to ring the bell towards four o'clock every morning."

"How do you mean, 'somebody'? It was a bonze surely?"

"I do not know whether it was a bonze or not.

---

[1] Japanese kimono worn in summer.
[2] Soya paste with the constituency and color of cheese.

At any rate, one could make out a faint 'ding-dong' from among the bamboos. On winter mornings, when a thick layer of frost had formed, while I was avoiding the general cold under my futon, the few centimeters of fabric of which gave some protection, I heard this 'ding-dong' echoing from the bamboo grove. I could not make out who was striking the bell. Each time I passed in front of the temple I saw the long paved roadway, the dilapidated door and the big bamboo grove which dominated the scene, but I never once looked inside the temple. I was content to listen to the echo of the bells which were being sounded from beyond the bamboo grove, and I huddled under my quilt like a shrimp."

"Like a shrimp?"

"Yes, like a shrimp—and I was murmuring under my breath 'ding dong!'"

"That's strange."

"Then, the tofu seller near the temple suddenly woke up and opened the shutters, and I heard the noise made by the mortar as he was washing the soya. And the rushing of the rinsing water for the tofu."

'Where was your house situated, by the way?'

"Well—where I could hear these noises."

"But where, exactly?"

"Right next to him."

"Facing the tofu seller or to one side of him?"

"Well—on the first floor."

"The first floor of what?"

"The tofu shop."

"You don't say! Fancy that!" Roku exclaims in stupefaction.

"I am the tofu seller's son."

"No, really? The tofu seller's son?" Roku repeated in ever-growing astonishment

"Then, in the season when the convolvulus was fading and turning brown on the hedge, rustling when one tried to pull their interwoven tendrils apart, and when a white sheet of mist came down everywhere and the street lamps began to gleam, the bell sounded once again. Ding-dong! The clear echo rose from the bamboos. And then the tofu seller near the temple, on hearing the sound of the bell, closed the sliding doors."

"You say 'the tofu seller near the temple'—but you are referring to your own house?"

"Yes—that is to say, at the tofu seller's near the temple they were closing the sliding doors. And you could hear the ding-dong! I went up to the first floor to lay out my futon and lie down. The *yoshiwarage*[3] we had was very good. The people in our district appreciated it."

The "forearm" and the "saber" of the next room have calmed down; on the veranda on the other side a heavily built old man of about sixty years of age, resting his bent back against a pillar and seated like a tailor, is pulling out the hairs on his chin with a pair of tweezers. He seizes the root of each hair firmly and gives it a sharp pull, the

---

[3] Fried pastry based on tofu.

tweezers moving apart towards the bottom and his chin moves convulsively as in a somersault. It is like a machine.

"How many days does it take him to get rid of all the hairs?" That is the question that Roku asks Kei.

"If he makes an effort, he can do it in half a day."

"I don't believe it!" Roku protests.

"Don't you? Well, let's say a day."

"It would be too simple to be able to finish in one or two days."

"True enough. Perhaps he will need a week. Look how carefully he feels his chin while pulling out the hairs."

"If he goes no faster than that, he won't have had time to pull out the hairs before others have grown in their place."

"Well, anyway, it is bound to be hurting him," says Kei, by way of changing the subject.

"It certainly must hurt him. Should we not give him a piece of advice?"

"What advice?"

"To stop it."

"What business is it of yours? We shall ask him how long it will take him to pluck all the hairs out."

"All right. You'll be the one to ask him."

"I can't. You do it!"

"I can if you want me to, but it's not really important, is it?"

"Well, no. Let's give up the idea, then."

Kei generously retracts his own suggestion.

The noise made by the farrier, who had paused in his work for the first time, again resounds beneath the clear sky—bang! clang!—aiming, perhaps, to crush under innumerable claps of thunder autumn's arrival in the mountain village.

"When I hear that noise I cannot help feeling homesick for the tofu shop of the old days," says Kei, his arms crossed.

"But has the son of the tofu seller got like that?"

"What do you mean by 'like that'?"

"There is nothing of the tofu seller about you."

"Tofu seller's son or fishmonger's son—to become what one wants to be, it's enough to want it."

"True. Basically, everything is in the mind."

"It's not only the mind that counts. Who knows how many tofu manufacturers in this world have anything in their heads? That does not prevent them from remaining tofu manufacturers for the whole of their lives! The poor creatures!"

"What does count, then?" Roku innocently asks.

"What counts is—well—to want it."

"Even if one wants them, there are lots of things society does not allow, aren't there?"

"That's why I said 'the poor creatures!' If one is born into an unjust society, it can't be helped. Whether it permits it or not, is of not much importance. The main thing is to want it oneself."

"And what if one wants to be something

and still does not become it?"

"Whether or not one becomes it, is not the problem. One has to want it. By wanting it, one causes society to permit it," says Kei in peremptory tones.

"Yes, of course—if everything goes like clockwork! Ha, ha, ha, ha!"

"But up to now, I've always conducted my life along those lines."

"That is exactly why I said there was nothing of the tofu seller about you."

"Perhaps I am about to become like one. Ha ha ha ha!"

"If that happens, what will you do?"

"If that happens, it will be the fault of society. Whatever happens, I for my part will have done what has to be done to make an unjust society just, and if it does not learn the lesson, whose fault is that?"

"Yes, well—society, you know, there's this about it: if the son of a tofu seller can become somebody who counts, there is still a chance of somebody who counts becoming a tofu seller."

"What do you mean by somebody who counts'?"

"What do I mean by 'somebody who counts'? Well, high-born, the wealthy." Roku immediately gives his definition of somebody who counts.

"Yes. The noblemen and the rich people, but they still remain tofu manufacturers."

"And these tofu manufacturers ride about in coaches, have villas built for them and act as if they were masters of this world. That is the disaster!"

"And yet those people have to become real tofu manufacturers."

"That is perhaps what we want, but not what they want!"

"They will have to become that, willy-nilly, and that is how we shall have a just society."

"Things will be perfect if it becomes just. Don't put yourself out!"

"Telling me not to put myself out is not the right answer. It is for you to help me. If only they were content to ride about in coaches and have villas built for them, but they are outrageous oppressors, these tofu manufacturers! When one thinks they are nothing but tofu manufacturers," Kei begins to wax indignant.

"You've suffered from them?"

Kei keeps his arms crossed and is content to reply in the affirmative. The sound made by the farrier continues: clang-bang!

"That 'clang-bang' again! I say, have you seen what strong arms I have?"

Kei suddenly rolls up his sleeves and exhibits his dark arms under Roku's very nose.

"You've always had big arms, you have. And then, they are practically black. Have you been pounding soya beans?"

"I have been pounding and drawing water. Tell me, if one treads on someone's toes by accident, who is it who has to apologize?"

"It seems to me that in principle it's the one

who has trodden on the other's toes."

"And if one suddenly punches someone?"

"Then you're off your head for heaven's sake!"

"You think a madman need not apologize?"

"Well, if one can ask him to apologize, it is better for him to do it."

"So you would not find it surprising if a madman asked you to apologize?"

"Are there madmen who do?"

"These days, tofu manufacturers belong to that class of madman. They oppress others and then force them to bow down. Normally, it is they who should feel embarrassed. That would be the natural thing, would it not?"

"Certainly it would be the normal thing, only, if it is tofu manufacturers who are mad, there is nothing to be done but just to ignore them."

Once again, Kei acquiesces. And a moment afterwards, as if addressing himself, says:

"It would have been better not to have been rather than allow madmen of that kind to proliferate."

Whenever there is a pause in the conversation, the "clang-bang" noise made by the local farrier resounds throughout the tranquil village.

"That 'clang-bang' never stops! It reminds one of the bell of the Kankei temple."

"It's strange how it occupies your mind. Is there some connection between the sound of the bell of this Kankei temple and the tofu manufactures who are mad? When you come down to it, what road did you follow, you son of a tofu manufacturer, to become what you are today? Tell me a bit about it."

"If you really want to hear about it. But it has turned cold, hasn't it? What about going for a bath before our meal? Wouldn't you like to?"

"Agreed. Let's go."

Kei and Roku go down into the garden, swinging their towels from their fingertips. The clogs with which they have been provided and which have straps made of hemp bear the coat of arms of the inn, just as if it were a big town.

Chapter II

"What use is this water?" asks Kei, the tofu seller's son, swirling the water around in the bath.

"What use is it? According to the formula, it should be suitable for everything. But you know, you can go on rubbing it on your navel as long as you like, it still won't go into your stomach."

"It is extremely clear," says the man with the prominent navel, taking up some water in his cupped hands and drinking it.

"But it has no taste," he protests spitting it out on to the floor of the bathing establishment.

"It's drinkable," Roku says, drinking it greedily.

Kei stops cleaning his navel and looks out through the glass with an absent-minded air while, leaning against the edge of the bath, Roku, up to his neck in the water, is observing the other's chest.

"You're well built, you know. Really like someone living in the wild...."

"I'm not a tofu seller's son for nothing. If one's not big and strong, one can't fight the well-born and the wealthy. It's one against all of them."

"You talk as if you really had an enemy. Who is it at present?"

"Just anybody."

"Ha, ha, ha! You, at least, do not let it worry you! You look as if you know how to defend your-self, but what really impresses me is that you have strong legs. If I had not been with you yesterday, I should never have found the courage to come as far. To tell you the truth, when I had got halfway I thought of stopping there and cutting my losses."

"I realize it wasn't easy. But I did make an effort to make it easier for you."

"Really? If that's true, you're a good sort. But you must be joking! You're taking all the credit for it."

"Ha, ha, ha! Me, taking all the credit? It's only high-born and wealthy people who take all the credit."

"The noble and the rich again! They're certainly your *bête noire*!"

"It's true I have no money. But I am a tofu seller without compare."

"You're certainly that': a tofu seller without compare. A hefty fellow in the wild state."

"Tell me, what are those yellow flowers grow-ing over there, the other side of the window?"

Roku, still in the water, twists his head round.

"Pumpkin flowers."

"Don't be silly! Pumpkin flowers creep along the ground. That one's climbing up a stake as far as the roof."

"You mean, if it's a climber, it can't be a pump-kin flower?"

"But it's strange, isn't it, that it should be flourishing at this time?"

"Strange or not, 'pumpkin flowers flourish on the roofs....'"

"Is that a song?"

"Well, yes—I didn't intend it at first, but I found it becoming a song on the way, in spite of myself."

"It's because pumpkin flowers also flourish on the roofs that even tofu sellers ride in carriages. It's the very limit, don't you think?"

"That indignation of yours again! What's the use of getting angry like that here in the mountains? Let's drop it and climb up to the summit of Mount Aso and watch the white-hot stones shooting up out of the crater. But don't go and jump into it! I'm beginning to worry about you."

"The crater must undoubtedly be something quite formidable. I've heard that stones the size of balls are thrown white-hot up into the sky. They fly out over hundreds of meters in all directions. It must be sensational. We shall have to get up early tomorrow."

"Yes, I agree to get up early, but I ask you one thing: once we're up there in the heights, there'll be no more racing," warns Roku straight away.

"Well, at all events, we get up at six."

"At six o'clock!"

"One gets up at six, finishes bathing at seven thirty, breakfasts at eight, finishes dressing at eight thirty. Then one leaves the inn and, at eleven, goes on a pilgrimage to the sanctuary of Aso, and begins the assent at midday."

"Yes, but who does?"

"You and me."

"You're arranging things as if there were no one but you."

"Come, come!"

"What an honor you do me! Just as if I were your servant!"

"Hmm! By the way, what are we going to eat at midday? Do we fall back on *udon?*"[4] asks Kei, taking up the problem of the meal the following day.

"No udon, thank you! Basically, *udon* consists of sticks of cypress, and makes you feel bloated."

"Well then, *soba?*"[5]

"No question of it. Noodles do not leave me satisfied."

"What would you like?"

"Anything, provided it's good."

"How do you expect to find good meals at the back of the Aso mountains? In the present circumstances, we shall certainly have to be content with *udon.*"

"What a funny expression: 'in the present circumstances'! What exactly are they, these circumstances?"

"The purpose of our tour is to invigorate our taste…."

---

[4] Wheat flour noodles.
[5] Buckwheat flour noodles

"That's the purpose of our tour? First I've heard of it. I agree about the 'invigoration', but there's no question of *udon*! I may not look it, but I'm of good social origin."

"That's why your resistance is so limited. When I was studying and had no money, I sometimes had to be content with a bowl of rice a day."

"You must have got very thin," says Roku pityingly.

"It's not that I got all that thin, but I was covered in lice. Tell me, has that ever happened to you?"

"Never! I am from a different social class."

"You ought to know about that. It's no easy matter to get rid of them."

"All one need do is put one's clothes in boiling water."

"Boiling water? It might do the trick. But one can't do one's laundry free."

"That's true. You didn't have a penny?"

"Not a penny."

"How did you go about it?"

"I had to lay out my shirt on the floor, then I knocked it with a round stone. But the fabric tore before even the lice had been crushed!"

"Oh dear!"

"To crown it all, my landlady noticed what I was doing and turned me out."

"You must have been on the point of despair!"

"Not really. If a thing like that had been enough to make me despair, I would not have survived this long. For from now on, I intend to

transform the well-born and the rich into tofu
sellers. And I cannot afford to despair over such
trifles."

"Under these circumstances, I too shall be
forced to walk along the street crying 'Tofu!' Who
would like some of my tofu?"

"But you are not a nobleman."

"Not yet, but I am not short of money."

"I'm sure you're not—but that is not enough."

"You mean I am not qualified to cry 'Tofu!
Who would like some of my tofu'? You under-
estimate my good fortune."

"By the way, could you wash my back?"

"Can't you do it just as well yourself?"

"If you want me to, but you know, the men in
the next cubicle wash each other's backs."

"Their backs are all much of a muchness. They
don't lose by the exchange, whereas our backs are
very different in area, and I'd be the loser."

"If you are going to engage in such complicat-
ed arguments, I might just as well wash myself
alone," says Kei. He stands firmly on his legs in
the water in order not to fall and energetically
spreads out his towel, slapping it into position at
an angle on his oily back. Then, as his arm
muscles suddenly stand out, the water-saturated
towel begins to rub to and fro over the fleshy
ridges of his back.

At each movement of the towel, he knits his
thick eyebrows in a frown and his nostrils dilate
and form a triangle, their sides moving firmly
apart. He tightens his jaws as if he were

performing hara-kiri, and his lips form a line from ear to ear.

"You look like a true Nio![6] It's the bath of Nio! How do you manage to make that grimace? It's extraordinary! I hardly think it's necessary to roll one's eyes like that when washing one's back."

Without saying a word, Kei rubs his back as vigorously as possible, from time to time immersing his towel in the hot water to saturate it completely. Each time Kei wets it, Roku's face is subjected to about fifteen drops of this mixture of sweat, grime, soap and hot water.

"I withdraw! You'll have to excuse me. I'm getting out of the bath."

Roku jumps out. But even though he has left the water, he is sufficiently admiring to stop and look at Nio's bath.

"By the way, who are the others here?" Kei asks from down in the bath.

"What do the other clients matter? You really do look funny!"

"I've finished now. Yes, it's very pleasant!" Kei exclaims, and lets go of one end of the towel to dive back into the water. The hot water filling the bath seems to have been taken unawares, as a real tempest arises from the bottom. The water goes splish-splash all over the floor.

"Ah, that's nice!" Kei repeats in the midst of the waves.

---

[6] A divinity, often represented by a statue with a ferocious head and in an upright position.

"Certainly, if one's as unrestrained as you, it must be quite pleasant. You've got nerve all the same!"

"Our neighbors talk of nothing but bamboo sabers and forearms. Who can that be?" Kei asks casually.

"It's like you, who are always talking about the high-born and the wealthy."

"I have good reasons for that, but what their motives can be nobody knows."

"For them it must go without saying. 'It was then that he received a hit on his forearm,'" says Roku, imitating the clients.

"Ha, ha, ha, ha! 'It was then that he dropped his bamboo saber,'" said Kei, imitating them in his turn. 'Ha, ha, ha, ha! They're not worried, those two!"

"Perhaps basically they're the kind who get angry easily. That often occurs in the old illustrated novels, you know. 'Thin gummy was in reality none other than the pirate Harimoto Kezori Kuemon.'"

"They have nothing in common with pirates. I had a look at them on my way to the baths. They were both sound asleep, their heads resting on the wooden head-rest."

"If one has a head that can bear contact with a head-rest, then, of course, 'one receives a hit on the forearm,'" concludes Roku, continuing to imitate them.

"They also lose their swords. Ha ha ha ha! One of them had left a red book open on his chest when he went to sleep."

"And with that red book 'one drops one's bamboo sword and exposes oneself to a touch on the forearm,'" says Roku, aping them to the very end.

"What was that red book?"

"*The Duel of Iga*," Roku answers without hesitating.

"*The Duel of Iga*? What's that, *The Duel of Iga*?"

"You don't know *The Duel of Iga*?"

"I don't know it. Is it a disgrace not to know it?" said Kei looking perplexed.

"There's nothing to be ashamed of in that, but I can't relate it to you."

"You can't relate it to me? Why not?"

"Why not? But don't you know Araki Mataemon?"[7]

"Hmm. Mataemon?"

"You know of him?" Roku asks, going back into the water.

Kei rises in the bath.

"Pity! No more Nio bath!"

"All right, all right, I will not wash my back any more. I get sudden flushes if I stay in the water too long, so I have to get out every now and then."

"If you are content to remain upright, I am relieved. Well, so you know him, Araki Mataemon?"

"Mataemon? Well, I have heard of him some-

---

[7] Samurai of the seventeenth century. Victor in *The Iga Duel* (1634).

where or other. He was not in the service of
Toyotomi Hideyoshi[8] by any chance, was he?" Kei
guesses at random, committing an awful howler.

"Ha, ha, ha, ha! I'm flabbergasted! For someone who prides himself on aiming at transforming
the wealthy and the noble into tofu sellers, you
don't seem to know a great deal!"

"Well, wait. Let me think a little. You said
Mataemon? Mataemon … Araki Mataemon!
Wait. Araki Mataemon. Oh yes, I know now!"

"Who is it?"

"A sumo wrestler."

"Ha, ha, ha, ha! Mataemon, a wrestler! That
beats everything, what a non-entity! Ha ha ha
ha!" Roku exults.

"Is it all that funny?"

"Anybody hearing that would laugh."

"He's so famous, is he, that man?"

"Of course. He's Araki Mataemon."

"I told you I had heard that name somewhere."

"Don't you know the saying 'At the end of the
exile, Sagara of Kyushu'?"

"It's a saying, no doubt, but I don't think I've
ever heard it."

"You're really beyond redemption!"

"What is there to redeem? I really cannot see
how not knowing your Araki Mataemon can
detract from my personality. Compared with that,
what I call beyond redemption is a fellow who

---

[8] Warrior and political leader of the sixteenth century. Kei
is thus wrong regarding the epoch.

gives up after five leagues in the mountains and never stops moaning."

"You're not going to talk about biceps and calves, I trust. Because in that sphere I have no chance. It's the one that belongs to the tofu sellers. I too ought to have worked as an apprentice in a tofu shop."

"I'll tell you this: weakness is your second nature. You have no will power whatever."

"I thought I had plenty. But I must admit that in front of a nice dish of *udon* my determination weakens."

"Ha, ha, ha, ha! The things you come out with!"

"But for a tofu seller you look just right."

"Black as I am?"

"White or black, a tofu seller is often tattooed, isn't he?"

"Why?"

"I have no idea, but at any rate he is often tattooed. And what about you: why don't you have a tattoo?"

"Stop all this nonsense! How do you expect someone as refined as me to lower himself to such a stupid level? No doubt it would suit a nobleman or a rich man, but not me. Any more than it would be suitable for Araki Mataemon."

"Araki Mataemon? You've set me a poser. I haven't so far thought about it."

"Never mind. At any rate, tomorrow we get up at six."

"Then at any rate there'll be *udon* to eat, won't

there? Perhaps my lack of will power is a problem, but the fact that your will is so unshakable is still more discouraging. Since we set out, I have not succeeded in doing a single thing as the mood seized me. I submit to your orders like a yes-man. One doesn't joke with tofuism, does one?"

"Obviously, if I didn't keep a firm hand on things, everything would be just happy-go-lucky."

"You're talking about me?"

"No—all those types who hang around; I don't know—all those people who like to hold the stage and who give themselves such airs."

"But you're going the wrong way about things. If it is I who have to submit to tofuism in the place of all those people, that's going a bit far. I can't get over such an idea: many thanks! I certainly won't be going on another trip with you!"

"That doesn't matter to me."

"It doesn't matter to you, perhaps, but it does to me, to some extent.

"On top of that, I am paying half the expenses; it's ridiculous."

"But you have me to thank for the chance to see the overwhelming crater of Aso."

"Poor man! There is nothing to stop me going up by myself."

"But the noble and the rich are such cowards, there's no doubt about it...."

"I'm penalized for them too! Look, stop getting me to pay for them. You must go to the rich and noble themselves."

"That's certainly what I mean to do one day.

They are cowards, they don't understand any-thing about anything, and as human beings they're not worth a penny."

"That's why they should be transformed, one by one, into tofu sellers."

"I am thinking of doing just that one of these days."

"You simply think of it, and nothing more—it's worrying."

"But if it's thought of unceasingly, then in the end it is carried out."

"What a phlegmatic attitude! Well, I know someone who, by thinking he would catch cholera, ended up actually doing so. I hope that's how it will work out for you."

"Look, that old man who was pulling out the hairs on his chin: he's coming along here, holding a towel."

"Take the opportunity of putting your question to him!"

"I'm getting out of here, because I'm simply baking."

"Come, come, and don't leave just yet. If you don't want to ask him, I'll ask myself. Stay for another minute or two."

"Well, well there are 'Bamboo Saber' and 'Forearm' coming along behind him!"

"Where? Ah yes—they are coming together. And behind them there's someone else. Look, it's an old woman. Is she going to take a bath here as well?"

"One way or the other—I'm getting out."

"If the old woman comes in here I shall be getting out too."

When they leave the bathhouse the sharp autumn wind blows into their sleeves and reaches their navels. Kei, who has a big one, sneezes incessantly. At the bottom of the steps, five or six melancholy-looking white hibiscus flowers stand out against the autumn twilight. There are dull sounds from the heights of Mount Aso.

"That's where we shall be going," says Roku.

"It's rumbling in anger—how exciting!" Kei replies.

Chapter III

"Sister, do you not think he's big?"

"He is very fat, it's true."

"Fat! But I am a tofu seller, you know!"

"Oh, oh, oh!"

"Does it make you laugh, knowing that I am a tofu seller?"

"It makes her laugh because being a tofu seller does not prevent you from having the head of Takamori Saigo.[9] By the way, with this *shojin*[10] food, I'm afraid we shall be able to climb tomorrow."

"You are still keen to stuff yourself?"

"Stuff myself? At this rate one could die from making futile efforts."

"No, no: we'll treat ourselves to this variety of dishes: *yuba*,[11] mushrooms, sweet potatoes, tofu,

---

[9] Politician (1827–77) who took part in the Meiji Restoration. It is said that his face was puffy and sullen, but no photograph of him has yet been found.

[10] Diet influenced by Buddhism, dispensing with meat and fish, and consisting mainly of vegetables and tofu.

[11] Product from tofu, obtained from the "skin" of boiled soya milk.

there are so many...."

"True, there are so many. There is even your source of earnings to be considered. That doesn't mean there is no problem. Yesterday I had to be satisfied with *udon*, and today there is nothing to be had but *yuba* and mushrooms. Oh dear!"

"Taste this potato. It has only just been dug up. It's fresh. Delicious!"

"It must taste flavorless. Waitress, is there no fish?"

"Unfortunately, there isn't any."

"'There isn't any'"—that's what always annoys me. Well, eggs, then?"

"Yes, eggs we do have!"

"Can you do me soft-boiled eggs?"

"What eggs?"

"Soft-boiled."

"You want me to boil them?"

"In a way, yes, but only lightly. Don't you know what soft-boiled eggs are?"

"No."

"You really don't?"

"I've no idea."

"I'm horrified."

"You're what?"

"It doesn't matter. Bring me some eggs then. But wait. Do you want some beer?"

"Why not?" replies Kei indifferently.

"Why not? But it's all you think of—drinking. Shall we go without it?"

"No need to go without it; let's drink a little anyway."

"'Anyway'? Ha, ha, ha, ha! I don't know any-one who likes 'anyway' as much as you do. Tomorrow you'll say, 'Anyway, lets have some *udon* to eat....' Waitress, bring us some beer too. Eggs and beer. Do you understand?"

"There isn't any beer."

"You have no beer? Do you hear that? They have no beer. One hardly feels one's in Japan any longer. What a dead-and-alive spot this is!"

"If they haven't any, we don't need anything to drink," replies Kei, again indifferently.

"There's no beer, sir, but we have *Ebisu*."[12]

"Ha, ha, ha, ha! Stranger than ever. Do you hear that? She says they have *Ebisu* that isn't beer. Do you want to try this *Ebisu*?"

"Hmm—why not? Waitress—this *Ebisu* of yours: it's in a bottle, isn't it?" asks Kei, at last addressing the waitress himself.

"Yes, for sure," she answers, speaking like the Higo people.

"Well anyway, uncork the bottle and bring it as it is."

"Yes, for sure."

The waitress goes away with a knowing air. On her exaggeratedly short kimono, with round sleeves and a pattern of interesting claws, she wears a narrow double-knotted girdle of chiffon. Only her hair is arranged in a curious Western style, leaving Roku and Kei bewildered.

---

[12] Japanese brand of beer, famous during this period.

"She's quite a character, that waitress," says Roku.

To which Kei replies placidly, "Yes I suppose she is."

He speaks without hesitation and then adds unexpectedly.

"She is simple and conducts herself well."

"Her taste is rather plain, though."

"Hmm, when a peasant mind benefits from a refined education, it produces a satisfactory personality in all respects. It's regrettable, all you need do is to take her to Tokyo and educate her."

"Hmm…. Why not? But first of all, one would have to remove the peel with which civilization has left her."

"But it's a very thick peel—it would be no easy matter," says Roku, as if referring to a watermelon.

"Hard task or not, it must be removed. Underneath their congenial masks, human beings are capable of every kind of baseness. If they are penniless, they stick to themselves. But if they have a certain position in society, that's when the problems start. They infect the whole of society with their meanness. A real calamity! And then it's among the upper crust and the wealthy that baseness is most frequent."

"But they are just the ones with the thickest veneer."

"On the outside they are quite imposing. But on the inside, compared with this domestic, they're underhand. It disgusts me."

"True. If I too joined forces with the austere…"

"That goes without saying. First of all, tomorrow we get up at six."

"And for our lunch we shall have *udon?*"

"We shall, at the crater of Mount Aso."

"But taking care not to let ourselves get carried away and finding ourselves at the bottom of the crater...."

"Face to face with that vital phenomenon of Nature at its most sublime, we must open our minds to the grandiose and rise above the cares of this world."

"But if you aim too high, you will no longer be able to endure the world afterwards, and in the end it will be all the harder to bear. Having said that, let us assume that one only aims just as high as necessary—I do not think I have the legs to conquer mountains."

"Unenterprising?"

The waitress comes in carrying a tray with a beer, two glasses and four eggs.

"And there is the *Ebisu,*" says Roku. "The funny thing is that this *Ebisu* is not beer. Well, will you have a glass?" he says, offering it to Kei.

"Yes. I should quite like a couple of eggs as well," Kei replies.

"I would remind you that it was I who ordered the eggs."

"You're surely not going to eat all four?"

"I am nervous about tomorrow's *udon* so I intend taking two eggs with me."

"All right, if that's the case, I'll go without them," Kei says, giving in immediately.

"I don't want to deprive you—take them. But for a member of the 'austere' set, eating eggs is normally a luxury. I'm sorry for you. Eat them."

"Waitress, where does this *Ebisu* come from?"

"Perhaps from Kumamoto."

"Oh, I see. The *Ebisu* brewed in Kumamoko is not bad. What do you think of the Kumamoto *Ebisu*?"

"Well, I think it's the same as Tokyo. I say, waitress, this *Ebisu* is good, but this egg is raw," says Kei, frowning at the egg he has just cracked open.

"Yes, for sure."

"I tell you it's raw."

"Yes, for sure."

"She doesn't seem to understand. Tell me," says Kei, turning away from the waitress and addressing Roku, "you asked for soft-boiled eggs, didn't you? Are yours raw as well?"

"If you ask for something half done, it will not be done at all. I'm going to break one open. Look, this one's no good."

"Is it a hard-boiled egg?" Kei asks, stretching his neck to look at Roku's table.

"Completely hard-boiled. Look at this other one. Yes, this one too—completely hard-boiled. Waitress," says Roku, turning towards her, "These are hard-boiled eggs."

"Yes, for sure."

"Is that all right?"

"Yes, for sure."

"It feels like being in a foreign country. You can

The Ikeda Station (now called the Kami-Kumamoto Station) where Sōseki arrived on 13 April 1896 as a newly assigned teacher of English at the Kumamoto Fifth Higher School. Sōseki stayed at Kumamoto for four years, three months. Two of his novels, *The Three-Cornered World* and *The 210th Day*, are based on his experiences in Kumamoto. (Photo courtesy Sōseki Museum in London)

Sōseki scholars in front of the main building of the former Kumamoto Fifth Higher School, now Kumamoto University. Sōseki taught English at the school for four years, from 1896 until his departure for England in 1900 on a government scholarship to study English literature. In 2001, the Kumamoto Sōseki Club was founded by Sōseki admirers. The organisers invite eminent Sōseki scholars to give talks. They also publish a newsletter. Photographed from left: Nishikawa Morio, Nakashima Saikichi, Sammy I. Tsunematsu, Nishi Tadaomi and Satomi Shigemi. (Photo courtesy Sōseki Museum in London)

Sōseki's study at Uchitsuboi House, now the Sōseki Memorial Museum, where he stayed for one year, eight months. It is one of the finest houses in Kumamoto. It was from here that Sōseki and Yamakawa left for their trip to Mt Aso. (Photo courtesy Nishi Tadaomi)

Kita-Sendanbata House. Now privately owned by Mrs Chiyoko Isogai, this house is the last of six lodgings Sōseki stayed in during his time at Kumamoto. He was here for only three months before departing for England. Sōseki's room and the exterior of the house have been preserved as they were originally. (Photo courtesy Sōseki Museum in London)

The Yōshin-kan in Uchinomaki, currently called the Sannokaku Hotel, where Sōseki and his travelling companion, Yamakawa Shinjiro (Kei), stayed at the beginning of September 1889 as they journeyed to Mt Aso. It was the setting for this exchange:
"Waitress, bring us some beer too...."
"There's no beer, sir, but we have *Ebisu*." [*Ebisu* is a brand of beer.]
The hotel has been preserved as in Sōseki's time. (Photo courtesy Sannokaku Hotel)

The Japanese garden at the Yoshinkan in Uchinomaki.

The 210th Monument in the *susuki* field. Sōseki and his travelling companion, Yamakawa Shinjiro (Kei), lost their way in this field as they made their way towards Mt Aso:

"Kei goes valiantly forward to where the clouds and the smoke lurk in wait. Roku, with a heavy heart, remains by himself, standing in the middle of the *susuki*, watching the back of the silhouette of his only true friend move off." (Photo courtesy Nakamura Seishi)

A present-day view of the volcanic Mt Aso in central Kyûshû.
"The crater must undoubtedly be something quite formidable.... One gets
up at six, finishes bathing at seven thirty, breakfasts at eight, finishes
dressing at eight thirty. Then one leaves the inn and, at eleven, goes on a
pilgrimage to the sanctuary of Aso, and begins the assent at midday."
(Photo courtesy Sōseki Museum in London)

see that the other gentleman has raw eggs and I have hard-boiled eggs."

"Yes, for sure."

"Why have you done it like that?"

"I boiled half of them."

"Ah, I get it! She's quite a girl, this one is! Ha ha, ha! You understood the meaning of 'soft-boiled eggs'?" says Roku, clapping his hands.

"Ha, ha, ha, ha! Simple if only you think about it!"

"You'd think it was a joke!"

"Have I made a mistake? Do you want me to boil the others?"

"It's all right, leave it. Tell me, how many leagues is it from here to Aso?" Kei asks, dropping the subject of the eggs.

"But we are in Aso."

"Yes, of course," put in Roku. "We needn't get up at six tomorrow morning. We'll stay here for two or three days and then go back to Kumamoto."

"Oh, please! You can stay as long as you wish."

"Since the young lady suggests it—well, when it comes down to it, what do you say? Shall we do that?" says Roku, turning to Kei. But the latter takes no notice.

"You say we're in Aso. But you mean the canton of Aso, of course?"

"Yes, for sure."

"Well, how far is it to the Aso sanctuary?"

"To the sanctuary—three leagues."

"To the summit of the mountain?"

"Two leagues, starting from the sanctuary."

"Right to the top—that must be terrible," says Roku suddenly.

"Yes, for sure."

"Have you climbed it yourself?"

"No."

"So you don't know?"

"No, I don't know it at all."

"If you don't know, that's a pity—I should be very glad if you could have told us about it."

"You are going to climb the mountain?"

"Yes, I'm very keen indeed to climb it," says Kei.

"As for me, I'm very keen indeed not to climb it," Roku replies, taking the opposite position.

"Oh, oh, oh! Then all you need do is stay here all along."

"Yes, I feel it's easier to listen to the distant rumble while lounging here in comfort. Don't you think the noise has become more violent than a little while ago?"

"Yes. It has got louder. It's probably because of night coming on."

"The mountain," she says, "is a little angry."

"Does it rumble violently when it's angry?"

"Yes, for sure. Then it throws up great quantities of *yona*."

"What is *yona*?"

"It's ashes."

The waitress opens the sliding door and rubs her index finger on the floor of the veranda.

"Look," she says, showing her blackened finger.

"It's true, it never stops coming down," says Kei admiring it. "But it was not like that yesterday."

"Yes, for sure, the mountain's rather angry."

"But you, you intend climbing it even if it's angry? In that case, would it not be better to put it off for a bit?"

"If it's angry, it's even more interesting. You rarely have a chance to see a mountain that's angry. It seems the fire that flares up varies greatly, according to whether the mountain is angry or not. Is that not so, miss?"

"Yes, for sure. It's very red this evening. Come outside and look at it."

Kei rushes to the veranda out of curiosity.

"Oh! It's very impressive! Quick, come and have a look. It's terrible!"

"Terrible? If you say it's terrible, I must certainly come out. Let's see.

"Oh, look at it! It's certainly very impressive. Under the circumstances, there can be no question of it."

"No question of what?"

"How do you mean, 'no question of what?'" If we climb up there, we shall be burnt on the way."

"You're talking nonsense. Things look like that because it's night time. In reality, it does that by day as well. Is that not so, miss?"

"Yes, for sure."

"'Yes, for sure', perhaps—but in any case it's dangerous. Even at this distance my face is burning," says Roku rubbing his cheeks.

"You always exaggerate."

"Your face is red too. Look at those vast rice fields beyond the hedge. The green leaves are all lit up together."

"You'll just say anything. It's the starlight."

"Between the starlight and the light from the fire, there's a certain difference."

"No, you really are ignorant. That fire is five or six leagues distant."

"The distance doesn't matter. The sky over there is completely red," Roku says, his finger tracing a big circle in the direction in which he is pointing.

"Because it's night."

"Night or no night...."

"You really are ignorant. It's not a serious matter when someone doesn't know who Araki Mataemon is, but not to know such an elementary thing is a disgrace," says Kei, looking at him sideways.

"Is it an attack on my personal qualities? I have no objection if it's simply that. But if it's an attempt on my life, I lower my arms."

"You're starting again! We only have to ask the waitress. Tell me, waitress, when the mountain is spitting fire like that, one can still climb it, can't one?"

"Yes, for sure."

"Can one really?" asks Roku, looking hard at her.

"Yes, for sure. Even a woman could do it quite easily."

"If a woman can do it, a man certainly must be capable of it! What a shame!"

"At all events, we get up at six tomorrow morning."

"I understand."

At these words, Roku comes back into the room and slumps down on the floor. After Roku's departure, Kei pensively gazes with raised eyebrows at the column of fire rising vertically from the nether regions to the vault of Heaven.

Chapter IV

"Hey," says Kei, turning round, "This is where we turn off to the left—and then at last we start our climb, don't we?"

"Is it here we turn off?"

"He told me that at the end of the road we would see the stone steps of the temple, and that we should turn to the left without going through the door."

"The old man at the *udon* restaurant?" Roku asks, incessantly rubbing his chest.

"That's the one"

"Do you think we can rely on what that old man says?"

"Why do you ask that?"

"Because there are so many occupations in this world and running an *udon* restaurant, in the first place, is a dubious one."

"It's a profession like any other. It deserves more respect than people who kill time by accumulating money and oppressing the poor!"

"It may be respectable, but it's not my style. But now that I have been forced to eat *udon*, it is no use complaining about it. Well, let's drop the subject; we'll turn off all the same."

"I can see the steps all right, but is that the temple? There is no pavilion."

"It must have been burnt down by the fire from Mount Aso. I told you. Look, the weather is becoming a little threatening."

"Come, come, don't be afraid, we have the blessing of Heaven."

"What for?"

"For everything, where there's a will, the blessing of Heaven is overflowing."

"You certainly have a nerve! First you call on the Austere Ones, then you join the Sect of the Heavenly Blessing. Next you'll be joining the Band of Heavenly Punishment[13] and become a Mount Tsukuba fanatic."

"But I belonged to them in the tofu shop period. They ill treat the poor. A tofu seller is a human being too. What amazes me, is that it is in no way to their advantage to ill treat them; it's just their way of passing the time."

"When did that happen to you?"

"It doesn't matter when. Tyrants have been regarded as wicked since olden times, but the twentieth century is full of the tyrants of whom we are speaking. Furthermore—and this is really detestable—they have a thick veneer of civilization."

"Perhaps it would be better if there were only

---

[13] An extremist group opposed to the shogun regime in 1863.

the veneer, without anything inside. After all, when one has too much money and is bored, one likes to play at being a tyrant. Give money to an idiot and he will usually want to become a tyrant. A virtuous prince like me is a poor man, and vile creatures of their kind only use money for the purpose of making others suffer. How hard life is! While we're about it, how would it be to put all those wretched creatures in a bag and toss them into the nether regions?"

"I'd throw it down—no doubt about that," says Kei, looking at the black curls of smoke and standing firmly on his two feet, shod in straw sandals.

"What vehemence! Are you sure everything is all right with you? Be careful you don't fall before you've thrown down the sackful of vile creatures!"

"The rumble is quite impressive."

"I can already feel earth tremors under my feet. Put your ear to the ground and listen."

"What's it like?"

"It's a terrible noise! Just as if it were roaring under our feet."

"And yet there's no smoke."

"That's because of the wind. As it is the north wind, it blows towards the right."

"There are too many trees to see clearly. If we go a little further up, we shall get our bearings better."

In a minute or so they walk into a copse. The path is not even a metre wide. Despite their closeness they are unable to walk side by side. Kei advances with great strides. Roku, hunching up his puny body, follows him in little steps. While following him, he admires his widely spaced footmarks. While looking at them, he lags behind more and more.

As the road zigzags up towards the peak, Roku can no longer see Kei. Less than an hour has passed since Roku lost sight of him. Peer through the trees as he may, he can no longer see any trace of him. Nobody is coming down the mountain. Neither does he see any other climber. There are hoof marks here and there. In certain spots wisps of straw from sandals have been caught on the brambles. Apart from this detail, there is no sign of a human presence. His stomach, full of *udon*, is beginning to feel tight.

In place of the clear sky of the day before, the mist had been causing them some anxiety since they left the inn that morning, but they had somehow or other managed to reach the Aso sanctuary in a light-hearted mood, in the vague hope that the weather would improve. When the clapping of the hands of the priest praying in the whitewood sanctuary sounded in the upper branches of the pine trees standing in solemn silence, something had dropped from the sky on to their foreheads. While they could see the white steam from the boiling *udon* filter towards the right through the tear in the paper of the sliding doors, they had thought to themselves that it might be the rain expected in the afternoon.

After walking about half a league in the copse, Roku notices the menacing clouds ready to burst, and the sound of the rain on the peaks rapidly receding towards the north. After this he hears a new sound of rustling leaves, likewise receding northwards. He bows his head and clicks his tongue.

After an hour, he reaches the end of the coppice. Or rather, it suddenly disappears. Roku turns round and, except for this single path that he has followed without looking elsewhere, he sees both to the west and east that the space is overgrown with grass, forming waves succeeding one another as far as the eye can see, and black smoke is rising in great gusts. The crater is out of sight, but the smoke is coming from it.

After leaving the copse, and less than fifty meters into the field, Kei, whose big shaven head can be seen, looks up at the sky. His umbrella folded, his close-cropped hair on his hatless head visible above the grass, he seems to be observing the geological structure of the countryside.

"Hey! Wait for me!"

"Hey! It's threatening. It's threatening, isn't it? Take courage!"

"I'm not losing my courage—but wait for me!" says Roku, desperately struggling through the grass. At the moment when Roku catches up, Kei fires a question at him:

"Why do you lag behind like that?"

"That is why I didn't want any *udon*. Oh, I feel

so poorly. What's happened to your face? It's all black."

"Oh, all right—but yours is black too."

Kei impatiently wipes his face with the back of the sleeve of his white kimono. Roku does the same with a handkerchief that he has taken out of his pocket.

"The fact is, when I wipe myself, the fabric gets blackened."

"It's the same with me. Look at the state of my handkerchief."

"It's frightful!" Kei looks up at the sky, exposing his monk's head to the rain.

"It's *yona*. The *yona* has melted in the falling rain. Look above those *susuki*,"[14] says Roku, pointing towards them. The long *susuki*, covered with ashes and dripping with rain, droop downwards.

"Yes, that's true."

"It's annoying, that is."

"Don't worry, we're nearly there. All we need do is go towards the place the smoke is coming from."

"That may be all we need do, but we don't know the way."

"That's why I waited for you all that time. We've just reached the fork in the road, where one has to know whether to turn off to the right or to the left."

"True, they're both roads. But seeing where the

---

[14] An Asiatic type of grass.

smoke is coming from, I feel it would be better to go to the left."

"You think so? I intend to turn to the right."

"Why?"

"Because on the right there are horse's hoof marks, while on the left there are none at all."

"Oh, I see."

Roku leans down and threads his way through the grass, but after five or six steps on the left he comes back at once.

"I don't like the look of this," he admits. "There's not a single footmark to be seen."

"No, there isn't."

"While there are some over there?"

"Yes, just two."

"Only two?"

"Yes, just two. Look, there, and then there."

Kei points with his satin umbrella towards the footmarks hardly visible under the *susuki* encumbering the road.

"Is that all? It's very worrying."

"No—there's nothing to worry about."

"It's the heavenly blessing, of course! But your heavenly blessing is frightfully doubtful!"

"No, no—it's the heavenly blessing."

Without leaving Kei time to finish his sentence, Roku's straw hat is carried away for ten meters by a gust of wind which suddenly causes the rain to swirl about. The force of the wind causes all the burgeoning flowers to bend over towards the other side at once, and there is hardly time to notice their change of position before they return to where they were before.

"It's quite exciting! One can see the traces of the wind on the grass. Look!" Kei points to the fleecy waves on the green grass.

"You say it's exciting! My hat has blown away."

"Your hat has blown away? That's nothing serious—your hat blowing away. Run after it. Do you want me to go and find it?"

On saying this, Kei throws his umbrella on to his own hat and dives into the *susuki*.

"Is it over there?"

"A little more to the left."

Kei goes further and further into the bushes. In the end, only his head is showing. Roku, who has stayed by himself, is getting anxious.

"Hey—all right?"

"What did you say?" says the voice coming from the half-concealed head.

"Is everything all right?"

Now not even Kei's head can be seen.

"Hi!"

Under his very nose, the black smoke, like a grey column riddled with spasms, mounts in puffs towards the sky, where, merging with the rain in the atmosphere, it falls pitilessly back on to Roku's skull, showing the direction in which his head has disappeared.

After a moment, fifty meters away, in a totally unexpected place, Kei's head suddenly reappears.

"Lost your hat?"

"I don't need one. Come back here at once!"

Kei straightens up his monk-like head and wades his way back through the *susuki*.

"Tell me, where was it that you let it fly away?"

"It blew away while we were still trying to agree on the direction. It's a pity about the hat but I have no wish to go on any further."

"Had enough already? But you haven't achieved anything yet!"

"With this smoke and this rain I am really terrified and no longer have the strength to go on."

"You're getting afraid already! Stop! Don't you find it exciting? That smoke coming out in puffs…."

"It frightens me, that smoke coming out in puffs."

"Be serious! We're going right up to that very smoke. Then we shall take a look inside."

"When you come to think of it, it's absolutely stupid. If we fall in after we've taken a look, that's all we need!"

"Whatever happens, we're going on."

"Ha, ha, ha, ha! 'Whatever happens'! Whenever you say 'whatever happens' you finally get the better of me. A little while back, too, because of your 'whatever happens' I ended up eating *udon*. If I now get dysentery, it will be because of your 'whatever happens'."

"It doesn't matter. I will accept responsibility."

"What good does that do me your accepting the responsibility for my illness? After all, you yourself are not going to be ill in my place!"

"Don't worry. I'll look after you. I shall be infected myself and see to it that you are saved."

"Oh, really? That reassures me. Oh well, I'll go on a bit further."

"Look, the weather's clearing up. At last, it really is the blessing of Heaven."

"Yes, it certainly is a piece of luck! I shall agree to walk, but on condition you give me a good supper this evening!"

"Once again you're thinking about stuffing yourself! Well, I promise, provided you get on with our journey."

"And then...."

"You have some further wish?"

"Yes."

"What, then?"

"I should like you to tell me the story of your life."

"My life? But you already know it."

"Going back to before the time you've told me about. To the time when you were a tofu seller's apprentice."

"I was never apprenticed. I was the tofu seller's son."

"Tell me what it was that made you hate the wealthy as soon as you heard the sound of the bell of the Kankei temple when you were the tofu seller's son."

"Ha, ha, ha, ha! If you are so anxious to hear about it, I'll tell you. In exchange, however, you will have to rejoin the ranks of the Austere Ones.

The problem with you is that you've never had any dealings with the rotten rich: that's why you're so carefree. Have you read Dickens' novel *A Tale of Two Cities* by any chance?"

"No, *The Duel of Iga*, perhaps, but not Dickens."

"That is why you have little sympathy for the poor. Towards the end of that book, you'll find the diary a doctor keeps when in prison. It's over-whelming."

"Oh, I see. And what is it like?"

"The diary tells how, before the Revolution, the nobles abused their power and made the lower classes suffer. I'll tell you about that too, after we've gone to bed tonight."

"Yes."

"You know, after all, the French Revolution is an ineluctable phenomenon. It's in the nature of things when the rich and the high-born abuse their power to that extent. Well, it's exactly the same with that force bursting out, with its dull rumble," said Kei, coming to a stop and looking towards the black smoke.

Piercing the autumn rain which still clothed the sky in mist, the thick swirling shape burst forth from a gulf a hundred leagues deep. The wreaths of smoke rose up. The noise produced by this thick shape was enough to make one think that the smallest of the particles of these great wreaths was trembling and exploding, leaping up from the distant bed of the abyss to vibrate above our heads.

Kei, dumbfounded, watched in the rain and wind, knitting his brows so that they looked like caterpillars, and said in an extremely ponderous tone, "It's magnificent, isn't it?"

"Quite magnificent," Roku repeats in completely serious tones.

And after a moment, he adds, "It's almost frightening."

"It certainly is," says Kei.

"The Revolution?"

"Yes, the revolution of civilization."

"What's that, the revolution of civilization?"

"No bloodshed."

"If you don't use the sword, what do you use?"

Without saying anything, Kei gives two little taps on his monk-like head.

"Your head?"

"Yes. Since the others have heads for a fight, I do too."

"Who are the others?"

"Those who make their most defenseless fellow beings suffer by means of their money and power."

"Oh, I see."

"Those who publicly trade on society's vices."

"Oh, yes."

"To defend their trade, they are always able to claim that it's for food and clothing."

"Yes."

"Those who publicly make society's vices their amusement—they must be punished."

"Yes."

"Including you."

"Yes, including me."

Kei turns heavily on his heels. Roku follows him in silence. What is to be seen or heard in the sky is smoke, rain, wind and clouds. The things that are to be seen on the ground are the blue *susuki*, the patrinias and the campanula flourishing here and there and sadly tangled with one another. They both enter the wilderness of desolation.

The *susuki* have grown so high that they envelop their legs and invade the path where there is already little enough room. Even trying to avoid them, they cannot go forward without brushing against them. When they do so, the wet ash brought down by the rain soils their clothing. Kei and Roku, in their white summer kimonos, their socks and their blue garters, make the saturated *susuki* rustle as they progress. Below their hips their clothing has taken on the colour of sewer rats: higher up too, with rain-dissolved *yona*, so that they look as if they have fallen into a drain.

At all events, even without the grass, their path already winds to such an extent that it would be difficult to find their way along it: all the more so in this proliferating growth. As they have already found it hard to identify the footprints, it must be said that they continue on their way trusting to the good will of Heaven for the outcome.

At first the smoke comes from the front.

Although it is difficult to determine the moment at which the path changes its direction, they are gradually subjected to the *yona* from the side. When the crater which they had seen from the side appears behind them, Kei abruptly comes to a stop.

"We seem to have gone wrong."

"Yes," says Roku reproachfully, stopping in his turn.

"What's happening? You look pitiful. Are you suffering?"

"To tell you the truth, I feel awful."

"Have you any pain anywhere?"

"I have blisters all over and I can't go on."

"It's annoying. Are you in any great pain? If you leant on my shoulder, you would find walking easier."

"Yes," Roku replies mechanically, without moving.

"When we get to the inn, I'll tell you something funny."

"But when are we at last going to get to this inn?"

"We're supposed to reach the thermal spa at five o'clock. Still, it's rather strange, this smoke. Whether you go to the right or to the left, you have this smoke in your nose the whole time, and it neither moves away nor comes any nearer."

"As soon as you start to climb, it gets in your nose."

"That's true. Shall we go farther along here?"

"Yes."

"Do you want to have a little rest?"

"Yes."

"You've suddenly lost all your energy."

"It's because of the *udon*."

"Ha, ha, ha, ha! On the spot, when we reach the inn, I'll treat you to my stories."

"I no longer want to hear your tales."

"Well, we'll drink some more of that *Ebisu* which is not beer."

"Hmm. Things being as they are, I doubt we shall ever reach the inn."

"Oh, we shall—it will be all right."

"The thing is, it's beginning to get dark."

"Let's see," Kei says with a glance at his fob watch. "It's five minutes to four. It's because of the weather that it's getting dark. It's a bit annoying if one's orientation changes to that extent. We've done two or three leagues quite satisfactorily since we started to climb."

"If you go by the blisters, we've done at least ten leagues!"

"Ha, ha, ha, ha! Just now the smoke was in front of us and now it is all behind us. We must be two or three leagues nearer Kumamoto."

"In other words, we're that distance further away from the mountain."

"That's possible. Look, close to that smoke there's another emission. That must be the new crater. When one sees that smoke rising in puffs, it seems to be quite close. Why can't we go there? It's bound to be just behind that hill, but as there is no road that leads there it's frustrating."

"If there were a road, it would still not be feasible."

"At all events, whether the cloud or the smoke, there is that horrible mass just above our heads. It's quite impressive. Don't you think so?"

"True."

"What do you think of it? The sight of such a landscape is exceptional. Yes, that completely black thing is coming down on us. Look, your head's getting some of it. I'll lend you my hat. Put it on. And you have a towel, I trust? Tie the bands underneath the hat so it doesn't get blown away. Let me do it for you. You ought to close up your umbrella. The wind simply gets concentrated in it. You can then use it like a stick. With a stick you'll find it a little easier to walk."

"That's a little better now. The rain and the wind are becoming more violent."

"That's true. A few moments ago it seemed to be clearing up slightly. The rain and the wind are one thing, but are your feet still hurting?"

"Yes. When we started climbing, I only had three blisters, but now I have them everywhere."

"This evening I'll crush some cigarette ash in grains of rice and make you a poultice."

"Once we get to the inn, everything can be seen to."

"It's when you walk that you have the problem."

"Yes."

"It's a nuisance, isn't it? If I go a little further

up, I can see whether there's a road being used by anybody. Look—you see that big grassy hill down there?"

"On the right?"

"Yes. If we go up there, we shall certainly have a panoramic view of the crater. And we shall then find our way again."

"So you say—but before we get up there, night will have fallen."

"Wait—let me see what time it is. It's eight minutes past four. We still have enough time before nightfall. Wait here for me. I'll go and have a look."

"I'll wait—but if you don't know how to get back again, it will be a real disaster. We shall never be able to find each other."

"Don't worry. Whatever happens, we are not risking our lives. If I'm in trouble, I'll call out to you."

"Yes. Call out."

Kei goes valiantly forward to where the clouds and the smoke lurk in wait. Roku, with a heavy heart, remains by himself, standing in the middle of the *susuki*, watching the back of the silhouette of his only true friend move off. After a little while, Kei's shadow disappears beneath the grass. The gigantic mountain rumbles more violently every five minutes, and each time the rain and the smoke seem to be quivering in unison, the final waves of vibration shaking the body of Roku, who remains motionless and deprived of strength. As far as the eye can see, the grass bends under the smoke and is whipped to and fro by the bursts of rain. Between the grass and the rain, great clouds roll at random. Roku, looking at the grassy hill, trembles. The raindrops, impregnated with *yona*, penetrate as far as his stomach.

The venomous black smoke moves in long eddies, and as soon as it is pointing upwards towards the sky, the earth under Roku's feet seems to tremble as if there were an earthquake. After this the rumbling of the mountain becomes relatively calm. Then he hears a call from below ground level.

"Hey!"

Roku cups his ears with his hands in order to hear better.

"Hey!"

There really is someone calling him. The strange thing is that the voice seems to be rising between his feet.

"Hey!"

Roku instinctively rushes in the direction of the voice.

"Hey!" he cries in turn, his lungs working to make his high, thin voice as loud as possible.

"Hey!" comes the reply in a thick voice from underneath the grass.

It is Kei without a doubt.

Roku, with a desperate effort, forces himself through the *susuki*, which come up to his chest, and perseveres towards the location of the voice.

"Hey!"

"Hey! Where are you?"

"Hey! I'm here!"

"Where are you?"

"I'm here! Be careful, it's dangerous! You may fall!"

"Where have you fallen?"

"I fell here! Look out!"

"I am being careful—but where did you fall?"

"If you fall, you'll hurt the blisters on your feet."

"It's all right. Where did you fall?"

"Here! Don't come any nearer! I'll come to you. Just wait for me where you are!"

Kei's resonant voice penetrates the ground and he moves gradually nearer.

"I fell, you know."

"Where did you fall?"

"Can't you see?"

"No."

"Well, all you need do is to come a little further forward."

"Hey, what's that?"

"Finding something like this in the grass is really dangerous."

"But how could there have been a ditch here?"

"It's the track left by a flow of lava. Look, it's brown on the inside, and not a single blade of grass has grown in it."

"That's really awkward. Can you come up?"

"How do you expect me to come up? It's at least three meters high."

"What a calamity! What are we going to do?"

"Can you see my head?"

"I can just about spot a bit of that porcupine's head of yours."

"Listen carefully...."

"Yes."

"Lie down flat on the *susuki* and then come just far enough to put your head over the ditch."

"All right. I'll do that. Just wait."

"Yes, I'll wait for you. I'm just here," says Kei, knocking his umbrella on the side of the precipice.

Roku, observing the situation, gently lies down on the wet *susuki* and nervously peers over the edge of the ditch.

"Hey!"

"Hey! How are things with you? Are your blisters hurting?"

"Never mind about my blisters, come up quickly."

"Ha, ha, ha, ha! It's all right. There's no wind down here. It's even pleasant where I am."

"So be it. But night is coming on. You must hurry and come up."

"Tell me."

"What?"

"Have you got your handkerchief?"

"Yes, but what do you want it for?"

"I grazed myself when I fell down, and a finger-nail was torn out."

"A fingernail? Does it hurt?"

"A little."

"Will you be able to walk?"

"Of course. If you have your handkerchief, could you throw it down to me?"

"Shall I tear it in strips?"

"I'll do that myself. Bunch it up into a ball and throw it. Be careful it doesn't get blown away. Make it into a firm ball before throwing it."

"It is so saturated that you've nothing to worry about. It won't be blown away. Well, here it comes!"

"It's getting dark. Can you still see the smoke?"

"Yes. The whole sky is covered in smoke."

"It's a terrible rumbling, isn't it?"

"Yes, it's got louder now. Can you tear up the handkerchief?"

"Yes, it's done. I have already cut off a strip to make a bandage."

"Are you all right? You're not bleeding?"

"The rain has made the blood saturate the sock."

"That must be painful for you."

"Oh, it's all right. If it hurts, that proves I'm still alive."

"I'm getting stomach-ache."

"That's because you are lying face down on the damp grass. That's enough now. Get up."

"If I get up, I shall no longer be able to see your head."

"That's a nuisance. After all, what about your jumping down here?"

"But what would be the point of my jumping down there?"

"Can't you manage it?"

"It's not that I can't—but what I am supposed to achieve by it?"

"We can go on side by side."

"Where to?"

"Well, this hole has been created by lava that flowed down from the crater to the foot of the mountain. If we go on walking along it, we shall arrive somewhere or other."

"Yes, but…."

"Yes, but you don't want to. If you don't want to, then it's too bad."

"It's not that I don't want to…. It's simply that it would be better if you came back up. Can't you try?"

"Well then, you walk along this ditch. I'll walk in the hole. We can then talk, one of us up and the other down."

"There is no road that goes the whole length of the lower level."

"It's covered in grass?"

"Yes. And on top of that, this grass…."

"Yes?"

"… comes right up to my chest."

"Anyhow, I can't come back up."

"You can't come back up? Well, well! well, well! Why don't you answer"?

"Oh!"

"Are you all right?"

"What?"

"Can you talk?"

"Yes."

"Well then, why don't you say something?"

"I was thinking."

"What about?"

"How to get out of this hole."

"But how on earth did you manage to fall down into a place like that?"

"I just wanted to reassure you as soon as possible that I was only looking at the hill. All of a sudden, I failed to notice where I was going and I fell."

"In other words, it's as if you fell on my account. I do wish you could get up again, somehow or other."

"Well…, it doesn't matter to me. It would be better if you got up. You mustn't catch a cold from the damp grass on your stomach."

"I don't care about my stomach."

"Are you in any pain?"

"Yes, I am."

"Well then, whatever happens you ought to get up. I'll think about how to get out."

"If you think of anything, you'll call me, won't you? I'll think about it too."

"Very well."

Their conversation breaks off for a moment or two. Standing in the middle of the grass, Roku looks anxiously about in all four directions. A black cloud descends on the distant hill and disintegrates half-way up. A mass as opaque as the sea surges one and a half meters from his head. His watch shows that it is nearly five o'clock. At this altitude it is darker than elsewhere. The whistling wind rushes unceasingly, and at each gust it brings black night from a distant land.

In the twilight, shadows lengthen and the storm rages like a whirlwind. The seemingly endless smoke rising from the crater is carried along pell-mell and spreads itself out as if dominating the tempest.

"Hey! Are you still there?"

"Yes. Have you found anything?"

"What is the mountain like?"

"Getting angrier and angrier."

"By the way, what's the date today?"

"September second."

"Perhaps it's the two hundred and tenth day."

There is another pause in the conversation. The wind and rain of the two hundred and tenth day invade the grass as far as the eye can see. It is impossible to make anything out beyond a hundred meters.

"It will soon be night. Hey! Are you still there?"

Not a sound comes from the man at the bottom of the ditch. It is as if the wind had borne him away. Mount Aso is rumbling as if its very bowels were under attack.

Roku, growing pale, once again lies down on his stomach on the grass, like a piece of wood.

"Hallo! Aren't you there?"

"Hallo! I'm over here!"

At the bottom of the little valley, fifty meters higher up, a vague white silhouette can be seen, and it seems to be beckoning.

"Why have you gone up there?"

"Because this is where I'm going to come up."

"You'll be able to come up?"

"Yes. Come here quickly!"

Forgetting both his stomach-ache and the blisters on his feet, Roku bounds like a hare.

"Hey! Are you there?"

"Yes, this is where I am. Can you bend your head?"

"How do you mean? It certainly isn't very deep. Well, if I hold the umbrella out to you, you can hold on to it to help you come out."

"The umbrella won't be enough. Look, I am very sorry, but...."

"What? You've nothing to be sorry about. What is it you wanted?"

"All you need do is undo your belt and tie it to the handle of your umbrella."

"I'll tie it like that. I'll do it at once."

"When you have tied it on, let the end of the belt hang down from above."

"I'll let it hang down. It's perfectly simple. I weigh sixty-six kilos."

"It doesn't matter how heavy you are. Come up, and don't worry."

"Is that all right?"

"Go to it."

"I'm ready. Oh no, that's no good. You mustn't slide like that...."

"It will be all right this time. That was just a first try. Go on, come up, and don't be afraid."

"If you slip, we shall both fall, do you realize that?"

"Don't worry at all. I just wasn't holding the umbrella right."

"Listen. Steady yourself by wedging your feet against the roots of the *susuki*. If you move your feet vigorously too close to the edge, the soil will crumble and you'll slip."

"All right. Don't worry. Come on, now."

"Have you planted your feet firmly? I have a feeling we're going to fail again."

"Eh?"

"What?"

"You seem to be afraid I haven't enough strength."

"Yes."

"But I'm normally built too."

"Of course you are."

"So calm down and trust me. I am a small man, but I think I can save a friend who is at the bottom of a ditch."

"Well, I'll come up. Heave-ho."

"Come on, just a little further."

Supporting himself on the *susuki* roots by his blistered and swollen feet, exposed to the rain of the two hundred and tenth day, and contorting his hips like a prawn, Roku desperately clings to the umbrella handle. Under the straw hat held firmly on his head by the towel, every part of his face, scarlet from the effort of pushing, is lashed by the wind blowing down from Mount Aso, while the *yona* falls pitilessly on his clenched, horsey teeth.

Fortunately, the handle of his eight-spoked satin umbrella is made of a strong natural wood with large knots, so that there is little risk of it breaking. It is to this curved natural wood that the Nassumi dyed belt is fixed and, like a new string attached to a robust Satsuma bow, it clears a straight path to the middle of the *susuki*, its end disappearing in the ditch. And from here, after a moment or two, up comes an enormous hedgehog's head.

He has hardly gripped the edge with both hands, crying out "Ah!", when the great animal's body emerges from the ditch with the umbrella attached to its back at an angle. At this exact moment, Roku falls over backward and crashes down to the bottom of the *susuki*.

Chapter V

"Come on, it's time for breakfast. Get up."

"Hmm. I'm not getting up."

"Your stomach pains have gone, haven't they?"

"Yes—almost. But in the state I'm in, I can't tell when I shall fall ill again. At all events, as it's the effect of the *udon*, I shan't be cured so easily."

"If you can talk like that, you're not in such a bad state. Look—what about starting out now?"

"But to where?"

"To Mount Aso!"

"You still intend to make the trip?"

"Obviously. To go to Mount Aso was the whole object of this journey. It would be hard not to go there."

"That's logical, perhaps. But, unfortunately, with my blisters, I'm afraid we may have to give up the idea."

"Are they hurting you?"

"Are they hurting? Even when I'm lying down, I can feel the pain throbbing in my head."

"That poultice impregnated with cigarette ash—didn't it work at all?"

"If fag ends worked, it would be a cause for worry."

"But when I put it on, you looked so grateful."

"Because I thought it would cure me."

"By the way, you really flared up yesterday."

"When?"

"When you were half-naked and pulling at the umbrella."

"Because you were so contemptuous."

"Ha, ha, ha, ha! But it was thanks to that I was able to get out of the ditch. If you hadn't got so angry, I might now be lying at the bottom."

"I pulled you along without worrying about crushing my blisters, and then fell half-naked on to the *susuki*. In spite of that, you don't even say thank you. You really are insensitive."

"But I still carried you as far as this inn."

"Not true. I walked here on my own."

"So you know where we are?"

"Do you take me for an idiot? 'Where we are'? We're in the village of Aso. To be exact, a place for changing horses, three blocks from the restaurant where you made me eat *udon* anyway. We've been climbing the mountain for half a day and now we've at last managed to climb back down again we find ourselves just where we started out. It's ridiculous! I shall no longer trust your 'Blessing of Heaven'."

"The reason why we were unlucky is that it was the two hundred and tenth day."

"And then you put on that performance of yours right up the mountain."

"Ha, ha, ha, ha! But you were quite moved at that moment and said 'yes, yes'."

"At that moment, perhaps, but now I think of it, how silly that was! Tell me, were you sincere?"

"Hm...."

"You were just joking, then?"

"You think so?"

"It's all the same to me, but if you really meant it, I shall have to warn you."

"But at that moment, who was it who was snivelling and asking me to relate my life?"

"I wasn't snivelling. My feet were hurting so much that I was desperate."

"But today you're on top form at the crack of dawn. You're a different person from yesterday."

"In spite of the pain in my feet. Ha, ha, ha, ha! To tell you the truth, it all seemed so silly that I decided to flare up."

"Against me?"

"Who else could have made me angry?"

"It was I who fitted the bill. By the way, if you would like rice soup, I'll order some."

"Why not? But first and foremost, I should be glad if you would enquire when the coach leaves."

"Where do you want to go by coach?"

"To Kumamoto, of course."

"You want to go back?"

"What else can I do? I'm certainly not going to share these horses' accommodation. That really would be putting too great a strain on me. Last night they were kicking the partition just next to my head the whole time. I was exasperated!"

"Oh, I see. I didn't know that. Was there so much noise?"

"If you didn't hear that noise, you certainly must belong to the 'Party of the Austere'. But you slept like a log. You had promised to tell me your life, come what may. You began by talking about the diary of a doctor but went fast asleep at the crucial moment. And snored terribly, too."

"Oh, really? I am sorry. I was so tired."

"By the way, what sort of weather is it?"

"It's a fine day."

"This weather's no use to us. It should have been fine yesterday, and what about you? Have you washed?"

"A long time ago. Anyway, get up."

"But I can't get up just like that. I'm naked."

"I got up naked."

"You're so inconsiderate. It's going too far, even making allowances for the fact that you come from a family of tofu sellers."

"I went out to the yard to wash in cold water. The proprietress brought me my kimono. It's dry. But it's now all grey."

"If it's dry, I'm going to send for it," says Roku, loudly clapping his hands.

The reply came from the kitchen in a man's voice.

"Is that the coachman?"

"It may be the innkeeper."

"You think so? Wait, let me try to guess who it is while I'm still lying here."

"But why?"

"I want to have a bet with you."

"But I don't bet."

"Come on, come on: coachman or innkeeper?"

"Well…."

"Decide quickly. He'll come in at any moment."

"Well, let's say the innkeeper."

"All right, you bet on the innkeeper and I bet on the coachman. Whichever of us loses will obey the other the whole day."

"I don't take decisions of that kind."

"Good day, gentlemen. Did you call for me?"

"Yes. Can you bring me my kimono? I hope it's dry."

"Yes, for sure."

"And then, I have a bit of a stomach-ache. Can you please make me some rice soup?"

"Yes, for sure. For both of you?"

"Plain rice will be just right for me."

"For one person, then?"

"That's it. And then, can you tell me when the coaches leave?"

"For Kumamoto, they go at eight and at one."

"Well, we'll take the eight o'clock."

"Yes, for sure."

"But are you really going back to Kumamoto? It has cost us such a lot of effort to get this far. It would be silly not to go on up Mount Aso."

"It just can't be done."

"But it has cost us such a lot…."

"How do you mean, 'cost us such a lot'? It was due to your decision that we've landed here. With these blisters, what do you expect to be achieved? Unless just to make the Blessing of Heaven null and void."

"If your feet are hurting, there is nothing to be done. But—what a pity it is! The decision cost us such a lot. Look, it's such fine weather."

"I tell you, we're going back together. It cost us such a lot to come here together, so we must at least go back together."

"But it was in order to climb the mountain that we came. If we were to go back without having done so, it would be unforgivable."

"Unforgivable by whom?"

"Unforgivable according to my principles."

"Your principles again! They're so narrow! Well, what about going back to Kumamoto and then returning here?"

"If we left and then came back, I would never forgive myself."

"There are so many things to apologize for with you! You're so pig-headed...."

"Not as much as all that."

"But you've never yet listened to me."

"Yes, I have—many times."

"No, you never have."

"I did so once yesterday. When I got up out of the ditch, I suggested continuing our climb, but as you insisted on coming down again, here we are."

"Yesterday was an exception. It was the two hundred and tenth day. On the contrary, it's I who had to eat *udon* so many times."

"Ha, ha, ha, ha! At any rate...."

"Let's drop it. We'll argue about it later, because the innkeeper's waiting...."

"That's true."

"Oh, by the way...."

"What?"

"I wasn't addressing you. I was addressing you over there, innkeeper!"

"Yes, for sure."

"Are you the coachman?"

"No."

"You're the proprietor, then?"

"No."

"What do you do, then?"

"I'm an employee."

"Dear, dear. Well there's no point, then. Do you hear? He's neither the coachman nor the proprietor."

"But what does it matter?"

"What does it matter? Oh well, it's of no importance. You can go."

"Yes, for sure. Do you both wish to leave by coach?"

"That is what we are arguing about."

"Well, well! The eight o'clock coach will soon by ready."

"Well, yes. We shall have found a solution to our argument before eight o'clock. In the mean-time, you can go."

"Well, well! Take your time."

"Hey! He's gone!"

"That's only natural. You told him he could go."

"Ha, ha, ha, ha! As he's neither the coachman nor the innkeeper. That's a nuisance."

"Why is it a nuisance?"

"Well, this is how I was thinking: Suppose he had said 'I am the coachman', I should then have won the bet. You would have had to obey my slightest order."

"I wouldn't have obeyed. I never made such a promise."

"But suppose you had made it."

"I did not do so."

"Let's assume you did. You would then have had to return to Kumamoto with me."

"Yes, perhaps."

"The idea appealed to me, but since he's an employee, it can't be helped."

"As he says so himself, there's nothing to be done."

"If he had said 'I am the coachman', I should have been prepared to give him thirty sen, the idiot!"

"He has not rendered you any service. There's no reason why you should give him thirty sen."

"But you yourself, the evening before last, gave twenty sen to that waitress with the curious head-gear."

"How do you know that? Her simplicity appealed to me. She deserves more respect than the high-born and wealthy."

"Here we go. Not a day goes by without an attack on your 'high-born and wealthy'."

"Quite the contrary—no matter how many times a day one repeats it, it's never enough. So much venom and cheek...."

"You're talking about yourself?"

"No—the well-born and the rich."

"Ah, I see."

"For example, let's say they attempt to commit an evil deed today, but do not succeed."

"But they shouldn't succeed."

"But they repeat a similar evil deed tomorrow. It still fails. So the day after tomorrow, they do the same thing again. They repeat it day by day until they succeed. For three hundred and sixty-five days or seven hundred days, they continue. They believe that evil deeds repeated ad infinitum transform themselves into good deeds. It's scandalous!"

"Scandalous!"

"If one lets them succeed, society becomes totally chaotic."

"If we live in this world our foremost aim should be to defeat the monsters of civilization and give some little comfort to the lower classes without money or power. Do you not think so?"

"Yes, that's true—yes."

"If you agree, follow me!"

"Yes, I am following you."

"Your solemn promise? Yes?"

"Yes, my solemn promise."

"Well, then whatever happens, let us go to Mount Aso!"

"Yes, whatever happens, we'll go to Mount Aso."

Over their heads the Mount Aso of the two hundred and eleventh day erupts, with a stored-up century of rumbling into the unending blue sky.

Titles by Sōseki Natsume

Inside My Glass Doors

Translated by Sammy I. Tsunematsu   ISBN 0-8048-3312-5

Originally published in daily serialization in the *Asahi* newspaper in 1915, *Inside My Glass Doors* is a collection of thirty-nine autobiographical essays penned a year before the author's death in 1916. Written in the genre of *shōhin* ("little items"), the personal vignettes provide a kaleidoscopic view of Sōseki Natsume's private world. The story is filled with flashbacks to Sōseki's youth—his classmates, his family, and his old neighborhood—as well as episodes from the more recent past.

The 210th Day

Translated by Sammy I. Tsunematsu   ISBN 0-8048-3320-6

The 210th Day, first published in 1906, is written almost entirely in dialogue form. It focuses on two friends, Kei and Roku, as they attempt to climb the rumbling Mount Aso as it threatens to erupt. During their progress up the mountain and during a stopover at an inn, Roku banters with Kei about his background, behavior and reaction to the things they see along the way. The book reveals Sōseki's gift for the striking image, as well as his talent for combining Western autobiography and the Japanese traditional literary diary.

Spring Miscellany

Translated by Sammy I. Tsunematsu ISBN 0-8048-3326-5

First published in serial form in the *Asahi* newspaper in 1909, *Spring Miscellany* is an eclectic pastiche—a literary miscellany—of twenty-five sketches, heir to the great *zuihitsu* tradition of discursive prose. These personal vignettes, which reveal Sōseki's interest in authentic, unadorned self-expression, are clearly autobiographical and reveal his kaleidoscopic view of his private world. There are scattered episodes from his youth and from the more recent past. Of particular interest are the accounts of his stay in England between 1900 and 1902.

The Wayfarer

Translated by Beongcheon Yu   ISBN 4-8053-0204-6

Written in the years 1912–13, *The Wayfarer* explores the moral dilemma of individuals caught in the violent transition of Japan from feudal to modern society. The protagonist Ichiro is caught in a triangle with his wife Onao and his brother Jiro. What ensues is, in a sense, a battle of the sexes between a couple forced to live together by tradition, a constant duel of two minds which allows for no finality. Ichiro's plight is not only the plight of the modern intellect, and modern man in general, but of the predicament of modern man in isolation from his family, society and culture.

Grass on the Wayside

Translated by Edwin McClellan ISBN 4-8053-0258-5

Completed in 1915 during a period of rapidly declining health, *Grass on the Wayside* is Sōseki's only autobiographical novel and the first book of its kind to appear in modern Japan. It is the story of Kenzo, Sōseki's alter ego, an unhappy, self-centered man. The book is remarkable not only for the depth and liveliness of its supporting characters—no modern Japanese novelist ever created as complex a personality as Kenzo's wife—but also for its treatment of Kenzo himself, who remains one of the most fully developed characters in Japanese fiction.

The Three-Cornered World

Translated by Alan Turney ISBN 4-8053-0201-1

In *The Three-Cornered World*, an artist leaves city life to wander in the mountains on a quest to stimulate his artistic endeavors. When he finds himself staying at an almost deserted inn, he becomes obsessed with the beautiful and strange daughter of the innkeeper, who is rumored to have abandoned her husband and fallen in love with a priest at a nearby temple. Haunted by her aura of mystery and tragedy, he decides to paint her. As he struggles to complete his picture, his daily conversations with those at the inn in the village provide clues and inspiration towards solving the enigma of her life.

Mon

Translated by Francis Mathy   ISBN 4-8053-0291-7

Mon is an intimate story of the consequences of an impulsive marriage, keenly portrayed in the daily life of a young couple and the quiet frustration, isolation and helplessness they face. Alienated from friends and relatives, living a lonely and frugal life, the wife, Oyone, placidly accepts their fate and blames herself for her ill health and their inability to have children. Sosuke, the husband, is content with their lives as they are. Things change when Koroku, Sosuke's much younger brother, comes to live with them. Not only does he become Sosuke's responsibility, but he also provides the impetus for Sosuke to finally re-examine his place in the world.

Kokoro

Translated by Edwin McClellan   ISBN 4-8053-0161-9

Written in 1914, *Kokoro* provides a timeless psychological analysis of a man's alienation from society. It tells the story of a solitary and intensely torn scholar during the Meiji era. A chance encounter on the beaches of Kamakura irrevocably links a young student to a man he simply calls "Sensei". The student gradually learns the reasons for Sensei's aloofness and withdrawal from the world, and finally the tale of guilt in his marriage and what he believes to be his betrayal of a friend.